CLEMENTINE ROSE

ROSE

and the Ballet Break-In

Books by Jacqueline Harvey

CLEMENTINE ROSE
and the Ballet Break-In

Jacqueline Harvey

RANDOM HOUSE AUSTRALIA

A Random House book
Published by Random House Australia Pty Ltd
Level 3, 100 Pacific Highway, North Sydney NSW 2060
www.randomhouse.com.au

First published by Random House Australia in 2015

Addresses for companies within the Random House Group can be found at
www.randomhouse.com.au/offices

National Library of Australia
Cataloguing-in-Publication Entry

Author: Harvey, Jacqueline
Title: Clementine Rose and the ballet break-in/Jacqueline Harvey
ISBN: 978 1 74275 757 5 (pbk)
Series: Harvey, Jacqueline. Clementine Rose; 8
Target audience: For primary school age
Subjects: Girls – Juvenile fiction
Dewey number: A823.4

Cover and internal illustrations by J.Yi
Cover design and additional illustration by Leanne Beattie
Internal design by Midland Typesetters
Typeset in ITC Century 12.5/19 by Midland Typesetters, Australia
Printed in Australia by Griffin Press, an accredited ISO AS/NZS
14001:2004 Environmental Management System printer

Random House Australia uses papers that are natural, renewable and
recyclable products and made from wood grown in sustainable forests.
The logging and manufacturing processes are expected to conform to the
environmental regulations of the country of origin.

For Eden, who loves to dance,
and for Ian, whose dancing makes me smile

SURPRISES

Clementine Rose Appleby bent down to give the lazy tabby cat a scratch under his chin.

'Hello Claws,' she said.

The beast rolled onto his back, closed his eyes and purred like a clattery diesel engine. Clementine tied Lavender's lead to the bench seat.

'Be a good girl. We won't be long,' Clementine said to her teacup pig and followed her mother through the door with the tinkly bell, into Mrs Mogg's shop. Today it smelt like warm pies, musk lollies and chocolate cake.

Margaret Mogg quickly put the caramel eclair she'd been nibbling onto a plate and under the counter. 'Good afternoon, Applebys,' she said, brushing her hands on her apron.

'Hello Margaret,' Lady Clarissa said as she headed to the far aisle to locate some baking powder and currants. 'Be there in a minute.'

'Hello Mrs Mogg,' Clementine called, rushing towards the old woman. The little girl's blue eyes were the size of dinner plates and she looked fit to burst. 'Did you know that the hall is going to be ready for Monday?'

Mrs Mogg smiled. 'Yes, and I'm very pleased about it too. Mr Mogg can stop moaning about my quilting group taking up space in the lounge room. I've heard that the garden club has already scheduled their first meeting, and Mrs Tribble is starting a new book club. There'll be Irish dancing classes on Wednesdays and the drama club on Thursdays.'

Clementine nodded. 'It's going to be busy.'

'And I saw Ana Hobbs there yesterday too, supervising something long and thin being delivered. I wonder what that could have been,' Mrs Mogg said with a twinkle in her eye.

'Yes, I wonder,' Lady Clarissa said as she placed her basket on the counter. She and Margaret exchanged knowing glances.

Clementine jigged about. 'It's the barre for the ballet school, of course!' she blurted.

Ana Hobbs was a famous ballerina who had recently retired from the royal ballet. Known professionally as Anastasia Barkov, she was starting a ballet school in the village hall, which had just been rebuilt after a fire.

Mrs Mogg leaned down and produced a red drawstring bag from under the counter. 'It's just as well I finished this yesterday.'

'What's that for?' Clementine frowned. She didn't need a new library bag.

The two women grinned at one another.

'I thought it might be useful to hold these.' Mrs Mogg held up a pair of white tights. 'And, oh, what else is down here?' Her forehead puckered and she put her glasses on the tip of her nose.

'My ballet shoes!' Clementine clapped her hands as Margaret Mogg passed her a tiny pair of soft beige slippers.

'I think they should go very nicely with this.' Mrs Mogg held up the most beautiful tutu Clementine had ever seen. It was red with a stiff tulle skirt.

'It's lovely!' Clemmie breathed. 'Please may I try it on?'

The women laughed. 'That's a very good idea,' Mrs Mogg said. 'Come around here and we'll get you changed.'

Clementine scooted to the other side of the counter, and a couple of minutes later she was dressed.

Lady Clarissa smiled at the sight of her little ballerina. 'Oh, darling, you look very sweet.'

'Hold on a tick.' Mrs Mogg disappeared through the door that divided the shop and the house behind and returned a minute later with a hand mirror. 'I'm sorry, Clementine, but this is the best I could do,' she said, holding it up.

'Can I have my hair in a bun for my first lesson?' Clementine asked, twirling around and admiring her reflection.

'I'll do my best,' Lady Clarissa replied.

'I've put some red hair clips and a ribbon in your ballet bag,' Mrs Mogg said. 'Oh, and one last thing.' She pulled out a tiny matching tutu from under the counter.

Clemmie gasped. 'Is that for Lavender?'

Mrs Mogg nodded. 'We couldn't leave her out, could we?'

'Oh, Margaret, you do spoil her,' Lady Clarissa said. 'Thank you so much. I could never have put this together myself.'

'I love it! We're going to be proper ballerinas.' Clementine put her hands above her head and spun around until she wobbled and almost fell over. 'Oops!'

Mrs Mogg caught the child just in time.

Clementine looked up and smiled. 'Thank you so, so much,' she said, hugging the old woman around her squishy middle.

'It's a pleasure, dear. I look forward to your first concert.' Margaret Mogg smiled. She helped Clementine back into her dress and stowed the ballet clothes in the red bag.

'Is there any mail for me today, Margaret?' Lady Clarissa asked.

Mrs Mogg checked the pigeonholes, where each household in the village had a slot. She handed Lady Clarissa a sizable bundle. 'Here you are, dear.'

Clementine looked at the pile. She hoped there weren't any nasty surprises. Her mother was always worried about how she would pay for things. 'Not more bills, Mummy?' Clementine asked with a frown.

'Not too many.' Lady Clarissa stopped at an envelope that she thought looked interesting. She slid her finger under the flap and pulled out a letter. Lady Clarissa scanned the contents and smiled.

'Have you won something?' Mrs Mogg asked. Everyone in the village knew about Clarissa Appleby's uncanny knack for winning competitions.

'What is it, Mummy?' Clementine asked.

'I think I'm going to keep this a mystery until we get home,' her mother replied with a wink.

'Ooh, that sounds exciting,' Margaret Mogg said and wiggled her eyebrows.

'Please can you tell us now?' Clementine asked.

Lady Clarissa shook her head. 'I think you've had enough surprises for one afternoon.'

'Enjoy your lessons, Clemmie, and don't worry if it takes a while to get the hang of things,' Mrs Mogg said. 'I did ballet when I was little and I'm afraid I was about as coordinated as a three-legged goat. I'm sure you'll be much better than I was.'

Clementine giggled, imagining a three-legged goat in a tutu. She held tight to her new ballet bag and followed her mother through the door with the tinkly bell.

SHOCK

On the way home, Clementine chattered non-stop about her beautiful red tutu. She couldn't wait for her very first ballet lesson on Monday.

'Do you think we'll get to do a show?' Clementine asked her mother.

'Maybe later in the year, darling,' Lady Clarissa replied. 'After you've had some time to practise.'

'I hope so,' Clementine said. 'Can I show Uncle Digby and Aunt Violet my tutu?'

'Yes, of course, sweetheart,' her mother replied.

The little girl raced off across their back garden and into the house, with Lavender running along beside her.

'Hello Aunt Violet!' Clementine yelled, kicking off her shoes by the door. She ran into the kitchen, only to find her great-aunt's chair empty and the room smelling of burnt onions. She unsnapped Lavender's lead, and the little pig trotted off to drink from her water bowl. Clementine was about to rush upstairs when a voice stopped her in her tracks.

'Why are you fizzing like a shaken bottle of pop?'

'Oh!' Clementine gasped. She turned from where she was standing on the bottom step. 'Are you all right, Aunt Violet?'

The old woman wiped her hands on a blue striped tea towel. 'Why? Do I look unwell?' she asked.

Clementine shook her head. 'No, but you're wearing an apron.'

'Yes, and why is that such a surprise?' Aunt Violet pursed her lips.

'Because you never wear an apron and you're never near the stove and you don't know how to cook.' Clementine's blue eyes widened.

'Godfathers, Clementine! If Pertwhistle can do it, it can't be *that* difficult,' Aunt Violet replied.

Clementine didn't think that was a very nice thing to say about Uncle Digby. She wondered if Aunt Violet's new-found interest in cooking might have something to do with her mother giving Ana Hobbs some cooking lessons. Ana and her family had recently moved into the cottage at the end of the road, and Clementine was in the same class at school as the Hobbs twins, Tilda and Teddy. They had a big sister, Araminta, and their father, Basil, made films. He was due to start a film very soon about the history of Penberthy House, where Clementine and her family lived.

'Goodness!' Lady Clarissa exclaimed as she walked into the room.

'What now?' Aunt Violet rolled her eyes. 'Haven't you seen anyone cook before?'

Lady Clarissa sniffed the air, then walked over to the stove and peered into the large frying pan. 'Oh, those onions look perfect,' she said, sighing with relief. She had expected to see a blackened mess.

'Of course they're perfect. Frying onions is hardly brain surgery, Clarissa,' Aunt Violet retorted. She slammed the lid on the bin, where her first three attempts were hidden from view.

'Would you like me to take over?' Lady Clarissa offered. 'I gather Uncle Digby isn't back from the doctor's yet.'

'No. I've started it and I'll finish it. But I don't like to cook with an audience, so why don't you take Clementine upstairs and she can do her home readers or something equally dull.' The old woman turned back to the bench, trying to remember if she was supposed to put the meat or the tomatoes in next. She'd thrown a tea towel over the cookbook and wasn't planning to consult it again until her niece was out of sight.

Lady Clarissa unpacked the groceries from her basket and placed the mail on the sideboard. She'd hoped to make herself a cup of tea and have Clementine do her homework at the kitchen table but she didn't want to upset Aunt Violet. Having her help out in the kitchen could be useful, particularly when they were busy with guests.

'Would you like to see my tutu, Aunt Violet?' Clementine asked. 'Lavender has one too.'

'Not now, Clementine. Can't you see that I'm busy?' the old woman snapped.

Clementine turned away and pulled a face. 'Mummy, can I show Uncle Digby when he gets home? He's *never* too busy.'

'Yes, of course. Aunt Violet might even be finished with dinner by then, so you can show her as well. I'm sure she'd *love* to see it,' Lady Clarissa said loudly.

But Aunt Violet wasn't listening. She was peering under the tea towel and wondering how long it was going to take to cook five hundred grams of minced steak.

TICKETS

Digby Pertwhistle peered at the plate in front of him. Spirals of pasta floated between chunks of meat in red sauce. There were some unidentifiable white-ish lumps too, which he hoped were cheese. The man leaned over and inhaled deeply, then coughed and spluttered. He reached for his glass of water.

'It smells . . . delicious,' he said, although he had his doubts after he'd noticed Pharaoh, Aunt Violet's sphinx cat, and Lavender bypass some stray drops of sauce on the floor.

Uncle Digby cleared his throat and glanced at Clementine, who had just caught an overpowering whiff of pepper too.

Aunt Violet stiffened. 'Eat up, everyone. You don't want it getting cold.'

Lady Clarissa, Uncle Digby and Clementine all dug in.

'Mmm, this is yummy,' Clementine said loudly as she chewed on the rubbery pasta.

Earlier, while banished upstairs, she and her mother and Uncle Digby had all agreed that they would praise Aunt Violet's efforts no matter what. It was a huge step that she had voluntarily cooked a meal and, even if it wasn't the best, she could get better with practise. In the past couple of months Aunt Violet had turned a corner and, instead of expecting to be waited on hand and foot, she'd been helping out quite a bit, much to everyone's delight.

Lady Clarissa and Uncle Digby looked at one another, their mouths full.

Aunt Violet picked up her fork and plunged it into the swirls. She was chewing slowly when all of a sudden she spat the whole lot into her napkin. 'Godfathers, that is *disgusting*!' Aunt Violet wailed. 'What did you do to it, Pertwhistle?'

'I didn't touch it,' Uncle Digby protested.

'It's just a little bit salty, that's all,' Lady Clarissa said kindly. She had been doing her best to keep eating.

'Don't try to make me feel better, Clarissa. If that's only a little bit salty, then I'm only a little bit stylish – and we all know *that's* a lie.' Aunt Violet pushed back her chair and marched over to the kitchen bench, where she flipped open the recipe book and scanned the ingredients.

Meanwhile, the others gulped down water and nibbled on bread rolls to get rid of the terrible taste.

'The recipe must be wrong,' Aunt Violet blustered. 'I did exactly what it said.'

'May I have a look?' Lady Clarissa asked.

Aunt Violet plonked the book on the table. 'See for yourself.'

Lady Clarissa ran her finger down the list of ingredients and stopped at the salt. 'Half a teaspoon of salt,' she read aloud.

'Yes, I know. Half a tablespoon of salt,' Aunt Violet repeated.

Lady Clarissa and Uncle Digby looked at each other and smiled.

'What are you smirking at?' Aunt Violet demanded.

'Mummy said "teaspoon", Aunt Violet, and you said "tablespoon". Everyone knows that's much bigger than a teaspoon,' Clementine pointed out.

'Let me see that!' Aunt Violet snatched the recipe book out of her niece's hands and peered at the list. 'Here it is. It says t-s-p, which is short for –' Aunt Violet pressed the heel of her hand on her forehead – 'teaspoon.'

'See, Mummy was right.' Clementine's eyes widened.

Aunt Violet picked up her and Uncle Digby's plates, stomped over to the bin and up-ended their contents.

'Aunt Violet, please don't be upset. I'm sure that if it was a little bit less salty it would have been absolutely perfect,' Lady Clarissa said, trying to calm her aunt.

The old woman walked back to the table and took Clementine's and her mother's plates, dumped the pasta in the bin and the plates in the sink then dusted her hands. 'Looks like eggs for dinner,' Aunt Violet said.

'Would you like some help?' Uncle Digby asked.

'No,' Aunt Violet replied. 'Because I'm not making another thing.' She stormed over to the table and sat down.

'Maybe you can have some cooking lessons with Ana,' Clementine suggested.

Aunt Violet shook her head. 'No, Clementine. I've said it before and I'll say it again. Some people were born to cook and others were born to eat, and I fall into the latter category.'

Uncle Digby stood up. 'Well, who'd like googy-eggs and soldiers?'

'Yes, please!' Clementine nodded. 'But not too much salt.'

Aunt Violet glared at the child.

An uneasy silence settled over the table. A few seconds later Clementine remembered something. 'Mummy, what was that letter about at the shop?' She pointed at the envelope that was propped against the vase of camellias on the sideboard.

'Why don't you go and get it?' Lady Clarissa said, grateful for the distraction.

Clementine sped to the sideboard and handed her mother the envelope.

'Well,' Clarissa said, 'it seems I've won a competition.'

Clementine clapped her hands together. 'Is it a cruise?'

'Not this time.'

'Is it a new car? You could give it to Uncle Digby,' Clementine suggested.

'Steady on there,' said the old man. 'What's wrong with my car?'

'It breaks down, Uncle Digby, and it's got

a funny steering wheel.' Clementine held her hands out wide, pretending to drive the ancient Morris Minor.

'I hope it's that new wardrobe of clothes for me,' Aunt Violet said, remembering the competition in the fashion magazine her niece had entered on her behalf. She was already imagining a row of new trousers and blouses hanging in her wardrobe. And shoes – oh, how she would have loved some new shoes!

Lady Clarissa shook her head.

'You can stop keeping us in suspense,' Aunt Violet snapped.

'I'm afraid you're all wrong. It's two tickets to see the Royal Ballet's production of *Swan Lake*,' Lady Clarissa announced.

Clementine's eyes lit up. 'The ballet!'

'Oh, is that all?' Aunt Violet barely disguised the disappointment in her voice.

'Mummy, please may I go?' Clementine begged.

'Yes, of course, darling,' Lady Clarissa replied. 'The question is, who would you like to take with you?'

'But I want everyone to come,' the child said.

'Sorry, Clemmie, I only have two tickets and I really can't afford to buy any at the moment,' her mother explained.

Clementine looked at Uncle Digby, who was standing at the bench buttering some toast, then at her mother and Aunt Violet, who were sitting at the table.

'I don't think Uncle Digby would like the ballet that much, and if he falls asleep he might snore and ruin the show,' she reasoned. 'And, Mummy, you'll probably have guests to look after. So I think I'd like to take . . . Aunt Violet.'

The old woman frowned at the child. 'Really? You want me to go with you?'

Clementine nodded. 'You said you love ballet, and you were the only one who knew that Ana was a famous ballerina.'

'Oh, Clementine.' Aunt Violet could feel a lump in the back of her throat. 'Are you sure, Clarissa?'

Lady Clarissa nodded. 'Of course. The tickets are for Saturday week.'

'Godfathers, what will I wear?' Aunt Violet leapt out of her chair and made a beeline for the back stairs. On the way, she snatched a tissue from the sideboard and brushed the side of her face.

'Why is Aunt Violet crying, Mummy?' Clementine asked.

'I think she's happy, Clementine.' Lady Clarissa smiled. 'Very happy.'

Clementine frowned. 'Grown-ups are so confusing.'

THE LONGEST DAY

Clemmie looked at the clock on the classroom wall. She'd been learning to tell the time and knew that when the little hand was on the three and the big hand was on the twelve, it was time to go home. She must have checked it at least fifty times already, but the minutes seemed to be ticking by slower than ever.

At least it was now after lunch, and the class was busy drawing African animals to add to the giant scene that their teacher, Mr Smee, had painted on the back wall.

'What have you got there, Clementine?' he asked.

'It's a lion,' Clementine replied.

Her teacher frowned. 'Are you sure?'

Clementine looked down and realised that her lion had very big ears and a trunk as well as a mane. 'Oops,' she said, her ears turning pink. 'That's silly.'

'Never mind, you can get another sheet of paper and start again if you like,' Mr Smee said. 'What's got you so distracted today?'

'Ballet,' Clementine confessed. 'It's our first lesson this afternoon. Tilda, Teddy, Poppy, Sophie and me are all going.'

'I remember going to my first soccer practice when I was your age,' Mr Smee said with a grin. 'I couldn't concentrate on anything all day.'

Clementine smiled at her teacher. 'You know a lot about kids, Mr Smee,' she said.

'Thanks, Clemmie. And, don't worry, there's only another half an hour until home time.' Mr Smee winked at her as he walked off to see what the children at the next table had drawn.

Clementine turned to Tilda. 'Are you excited about this afternoon?'

The child nodded. 'I'm happy that Mummy can start the ballet school. Daddy said he was going to have to send her back to work if she didn't get started soon. He says that she can't sit still.'

'You're lucky to have a mum who's a ballerina,' Clementine said.

Tilda smiled. 'And you're lucky to have a mum who can cook.'

Joshua Tribble overheard the girls talking. 'Ballet's stupid.'

Clementine glared at him. 'No, it's not!'

'It's just for sissy girls,' Joshua teased.

'That's not true,' Tilda said. 'Teddy does ballet and he's really good, and Mummy said that there are other boys enrolled in the classes too.'

'Is Teddy going to wear tights and flap around like a fairy?' Joshua mocked, fluttering his arms as if they were wings.

Teddy glanced up from where he was sitting on the other side of the cluster of tables. 'No,' he said. 'Ballet dancers are really strong and sometimes they have to lift the ballerinas up with one hand.'

Joshua laughed nastily. 'Boys who do ballet aren't allowed to play soccer.'

'Since when?' Clementine narrowed her eyes at him. 'If you don't stop being mean, Joshua, I'm telling Mr Smee.'

'I don't care. He thinks boys who do ballet are stupid too.' Joshua wrinkled his nose and stuck out his tongue.

Roderick Smee looked across from the far side of the room and wondered what Clementine had done to deserve being on the receiving end of Joshua's lizard-like tongue.

'Hey, Josh, what's that for?' he called out.

'Joshua said that boys who do ballet are fairies,' Clementine said.

'I didn't say they *are* fairies. I said that they flap around *like* fairies. Don't they, Angus?' Joshua looked to his friend for support, but Angus's cheeks flushed pink and the boy buried his head in his work.

'Joshua Tribble, come here,' said Mr Smee. 'Now!'

Joshua stood up and skulked over to the corner, where the children could hear Mr Smee telling him that he wasn't going to put up with that sort of nonsense at all.

A couple of minutes later Mr Smee walked to the centre of the classroom. 'Right, everyone, it's time to pack up.'

Joshua walked back to his table and pulled a face at Clementine, but she wasn't worried. Mr Smee might not have eyes in the back of his head the way Mrs Bottomley did, but his radar for 'Tribble trouble' was pretty good.

The children put their home readers into their bags and gathered up the rest of their belongings before Mr Smee said good afternoon. The class chorused the same farewell back to him, fidgeting as they stood behind their desks.

'Off you go, everyone,' Mr Smee instructed. 'Enjoy your ballet class, Clementine,' he called as she hurried for the door behind Tilda and Teddy and Sophie and Poppy.

'Thanks, Mr Smee,' Clementine turned and grinned at her teacher. 'I can't wait!'

FIRST POSITION

News of Ana's ballet school had spread through the district like wildfire. Her toddler class was bursting at the seams, and the group for five-to-seven-year-olds was almost full as well. It was starting to look as if she might need to hold extra classes on other days. The trouble was that the hall was fast booking up for all sorts of activities.

'Hello everyone,' Ana greeted her eager students. 'My name is Ana Hobbs and I'd like to welcome you all to our very first class. Now, if the girls would like to get changed backstage, the boys can get ready in the little room off the kitchen.'

Lady Clarissa and some of the other mothers helped the girls into their tutus and ballet shoes while Ana went to check on the boys. That didn't take long as there were only three lads, and their outfits of black tracksuit pants and white polo shirts weren't nearly as difficult to get into.

Clementine changed quickly and scampered back out into the hall, where Ana was fiddling with the stereo. She glanced up and smiled. 'Don't you look gorgeous, Clemmie. Have you been looking forward to this?'

Clementine nodded. 'Did you know Mummy won two tickets to see *Swan Lake* at the opera house and Aunt Violet is taking me on Saturday?' Clementine jigged about excitedly. 'So I get to *do* ballet and *see* ballet too.'

'That's wonderful,' Ana said. 'I have lots of friends dancing in that production. Keep an eye out for the baddie in black, Von Rothbart.

The man playing him is called Sean, and he, his wife and their boys are coming to visit in a few weeks' time. We can't fit them all in our house, so they'll be staying at your hotel.'

'How old are the boys?' Clementine asked. She loved it when children came to stay.

'Dash is eleven and Max is seven,' Ana replied. 'They're bags of fun. Mintie and the twins adore them.' Clementine had given Ana an idea. She wouldn't say anything just yet but she'd make a call when she got home. She glanced around at the children. 'Well, it looks like everyone's ready. Shall we make a start? Boys, would you like to join us?'

The three lads had been charging about at the far end of the hall, kicking a scrunched-up ball of paper. Reluctantly, they ended their game and gathered at the back of the group.

Six little girls in matching red tutus, beige ballet shoes and with their hair pulled back into buns, awaited their first instructions. Clementine knew Poppy, Tilda and Sophie, and she recognised the other two girls who were in

Kindergarten at her school, though she wasn't sure of their names.

'Hello Angus.' Clementine waved at the boy who was standing behind her. He gave a half-wave back. 'I didn't know you were doing ballet.'

'Mum made me.' He lowered his eyes. 'Don't tell anyone at school, okay?'

'Okay.' Clementine frowned. 'Are you worried because of what Joshua said?'

'No,' Angus replied with a shake of his head. 'It's just no one else's business. And tell *them* not to say anything, either.' Angus pointed at the other children from their class.

The parents had all disappeared. When the children were enrolled, Ana had made it very clear that she preferred to teach without an audience and she believed it was better for the students too. Lady Clarissa and Odette Rousseau, Sophie's mother, took the opportunity to walk over to Penberthy House for a cup of tea.

Ana pressed a button on the stereo and a pop song blared from its speakers. 'Now, children, the first thing we're going to do is warm up.'

She put her hands on her hips and jumped up and down on the spot. The children all did the same. Ana counted the beats out loud for them all to keep time. When she skipped in a circle, the children copied her perfectly. Ana then turned off the music and asked the children to form two lines in front of her.

'One of the most important things you need to learn in ballet is how to stand,' Ana said. She put her heels together and turned out her toes, creating a straight line with her feet. 'I don't expect you will be able to get your feet out this far on your first try, but let's see how everyone goes.'

Clementine turned out her left foot and then her right. She wobbled for a moment, then stiffened her legs and stood as still as she could.

'That's fabulous, Clementine!' Ana smiled, and the girl grinned back.

Poppy couldn't turn out her feet quite as far, but Ana praised her efforts too. Tilda, who'd been having lessons for a while, was amazing.

'Well done, Angus,' Ana commended the boy. 'You're a natural.'

The lad's cheeks lit up and he looked down at the floor. The other little boy, Gareth, was in Kindergarten at Clementine's school. He twirled around and sat on the floor and didn't even try to do anything Ana said.

The children, except for Gareth, held their places. Ana walked back to the front and put her hands down in a soft semicircle.

'Can everyone do this with their arms?' she asked. 'Imagine you're hugging a giant ball, then turn out your feet. We call this first position. Now I want you all to relax. When I say "first position", let's see who can do it again.'

Tilda looked like an expert while the other children wobbled and swayed into position. Clementine tried to imagine she was holding the beach ball she and Freddy played with on holidays earlier in the year.

Ana turned on the stereo, but this time it was soft music played by an orchestra that filled the room. 'This music is from a very famous ballet called *Swan Lake*,' she told the class.

Clementine grinned.

Ana showed the children second position, then they did some exercises skipping in time to the music and pointing their toes.

'Are we going to learn twirling?' Clementine asked Ana.

'Twirling comes a bit later, Clementine,' Ana said. 'Does anyone know what twirling is called in ballet?'

The children looked blankly at one another before Teddy raised his hand. 'It's called a *pirouette*,' he said.

'Yes, Teddy, that's exactly what it's called.' His mother nodded and turned to the class. 'It's a French word. Can you all say it after me?'

The children nodded and echoed the word back to Ana, who smiled broadly.

'There are lots of French words in ballet,' she said. 'I think my favourite is *pas de chat*.'

'What's that?' Clemmie asked.

Sophie put up her hand, and Ana nodded at her. 'I think I know. Daddy is French and I think it means "step of the cat".'

'Well done, Sophie, that's exactly right. Clever girl.'

'Can you show us *pas de chat*?' Clemmie asked.

Ana smiled. 'Why not?'

She hopped up and put on some music, then stood with her hands softly in front of her. Ana raised them up slowly then leapt three steps to the left and then three steps to the right.

The children all began to imitate her, leaping left and then right.

'Softly, softly,' Ana reminded them. Some of the children resembled baby hippos more than cats.

Ana glanced at the clock and was alarmed to find it was already half past four.

'Goodness, I'm afraid we're finished for the day,' she said, switching off the music.

Clementine's face fell. 'No, that was too fast.'

'I take it that means you'll be back again next week, Clementine,' Ana said with a wink.

'I don't want to wait that long,' the child replied. 'I thought we would learn a dance today.'

Ana smiled. 'Oh, sweetheart, we have to master some steps first. I do have a surprise, though.'

Clementine looked at the woman expectantly.

'At the end of the month we have the official opening of the village hall, and we've been asked to do a short performance,' Ana said.

'Can we do a proper dance?' Clementine asked, jigging up and down on the spot.

'With costumes?' Teddy added.

'I hadn't really thought about that,' Ana said. 'Perhaps we could do a snippet of something that's not too complicated, though I'm not sure we'll have time to make special costumes, Teddy. I think the girls look lovely in their tutus but we could try to find something more exciting for the boys to wear.'

'We could ask Uncle Felix to make some sets for us,' Teddy suggested.

The children grinned at each other and pumped their fists excitedly.

'Goodness me, this is sounding bigger than *Ben-Hur*,' Ana laughed.

Lady Clarissa and Mrs Rousseau walked into the hall with Angus's mother, Mrs Archibald, behind them.

'Good afternoon, everyone,' Ana said as she dismissed the class.

'Go-ood af-ter-noon, Ana,' the children chorused happily.

Clementine ran to join her mother.

'How was your very first ballet lesson, darling?' Lady Clarissa asked.

'We learned first position and second position and skipping with our hands on our hips,' Clementine babbled. 'But there was no twirling and we haven't done any proper dancing yet.' Her mouth drooped.

'Never mind, it takes time to become good at something like ballet,' Lady Clarissa said.

Clementine perked up. 'But that's okay, we're doing a show for the village.'

'Oh, really?' Lady Clarissa said, surprised. 'Mrs Tribble mentioned she would like your class to perform, though I think she was hoping that Ana might dance too. I know she's lined up Mrs Mogg's quilting group for an exhibition and she was working hard to convince the new Irish dancing teacher to be part of the program as well.'

Beside them, Mrs Archibald asked Angus what he thought of the class.

'It was okay,' the boy said.

Clementine smiled at him and, although he was trying hard not to, he couldn't help but give her a small grin back.

'So you'll come again next week?' Mrs Archibald said.

Clementine looked at him, and the boy shrugged.

'You don't have to if you don't want to,' Mrs Archibald said. 'Your father and I just thought this might be fun since you're always dancing around the house. You could try the Irish dancing class if you'd rather. I heard there are some boys in the class.'

Angus shook his head. 'I'll stick with this,' he whispered.

'You were really good, Angus,' Clementine said.

'Thanks,' Angus said, and followed his mother outside.

'See you tomorrow,' Clementine called.

The boy turned and gave Clemmie a wave.

STORIES

The next morning Clementine raced across the playground to drop her bag in the locker room. She was on her way to find Sophie and Poppy when she spotted Joshua Tribble standing around the corner. He was humming to himself and jigging about from one leg to the other.

'Are you dancing?' Clementine asked.

The boy spun around. His face was the colour of a tomato and he shook his head. 'Of course not. Dancing is stupid!'

'Do you need to go to the toilet?' Clementine asked.

'No!' Joshua snatched up his soccer ball and sped away into the playground.

Clementine was left wondering what the boy was up to this time.

'How was your first ballet lesson, Clemmie?' Mr Smee asked as she walked into the classroom.

'I loved it,' Clementine replied with a beaming smile. 'We're doing a concert for the village to celebrate the new hall.'

Mr Smee raised an eyebrow. 'A concert already? That sounds ambitious.'

'Ana is going to help us,' Clementine explained, 'so we don't get too muddled-up.'

The children found their seats and Mr Smee waited for everyone to settle down before he said good morning and instructed them to take out their writing books. Each morning he wrote the start of a sentence on the whiteboard, which was sometimes accompanied by a picture, and they had fifteen minutes to write as much as they could. It was Clementine's favourite part of the day, and she was getting much better with her stories.

'All right, everyone, I want you to look at the picture on the screen and use this as your first sentence.' The teacher brought up the slide.

Clementine gasped.

'I thought you'd enjoy this one, Clementine,' Mr Smee said, smiling at her.

'What?' Joshua wailed. 'That's *so* dumb.'

Projected onto the screen was a stage full of twirling ballerinas and, underneath it, a sentence which said 'Seventeen dancers twirled across the stage . . .'

'I'm not writing about ballet. Ballet is for girls!' Joshua bleated.

'Joshua, what did we write about yesterday?' the teacher asked.

'Dragons,' the boy replied.

'And did you enjoy that topic?'

Joshua nodded. 'Yeah, because dragons are cool.'

'Well, today I want you to stretch your imagination and write about ballet. I like to choose things that are interesting to the class and at the moment I know this is a biggie.' Mr Smee turned to the class. 'Has anyone got an idea of what to write about?'

'I could write about going to *Swan Lake* with Aunt Violet,' Clementine said. 'She's taking me on Saturday.'

'That sounds great,' Mr Smee replied.

Astrid put up her hand and the teacher pointed at her. 'It could be a picture on a wall and someone is daydreaming about wanting to be a ballerina.'

'Another good idea,' said Mr Smee. 'Joshua – good to see you with your hand up.'

'They could all fall off the stage and the hall blows up.' Joshua grinned.

There was a rowdy chorus of approval from some of the boys. Joshua stared at Angus, who quickly nodded.

'I'd enjoy your stories more if they were less violent,' the teacher said, giving Joshua a stern look. 'What about you, Angus?' Mr Smee asked.

'Umm.' The boy hesitated. 'A spaceship could suck them up to outer space and the aliens could eat their brains?'

Several students cackled loudly.

'Perhaps you boys could try to write something a little more sensible. Maybe there's a concert and something goes wrong. What if the ballerinas start spinning so fast they can't stop? They could spin out of control, twirling all the way into the street and across the whole country.'

Joshua wrinkled his nose.

'Well, you'd better get started,' Mr Smee said to the class. 'See if you can try to write more than you did yesterday and remember to read over your work once you've finished. I'll come around and help anyone who needs it.'

Clementine started immediately and wrote about the dancers leaping and twirling across the stage. They even did the *pas de chat*. Once she finished, she checked over her writing and started to draw a picture to go with it.

'What's your story about, Angus?' she asked, looking at the boy sitting opposite her.

Angus shrugged.

'I thought you liked ballet,' Clementine said.

Angus glared at her. 'You're not supposed to say anything,' he whispered.

Clementine frowned at him. 'I didn't.'

'You'd better not,' Angus hissed.

'What's the matter? Are you having a fight with your girlfriend?' Joshua leaned over from the Cheetahs table beside the Warthogs.

'No.' Angus's face was red and his eyebrows were angry.

'What's up, boys?' Mr Smee asked.

'Angus is having a fight with his *girlfriend*,' Joshua teased.

This was followed by a titter of giggles around the room.

'Angus is not my boyfriend, Joshua,' Clementine snapped.

'Joshua, get on with your work.' Mr Smee walked over to see whether the boy had yet managed to put pencil to paper. He was surprised to see that the lad had written half a page. 'Well done, Joshua, but it would be great to have a picture to go with your story.'

Angus hadn't fared nearly as well. His page was still blank.

'You're usually full of interesting ideas,' the teacher said.

The boy shrugged.

'You can write about the aliens if you really want to,' Mr Smee offered.

'I don't care.' Angus picked up his pencil and wrote 'The Stupid Ballet' at the top of the page.

Roderick Smee looked at the lad. Something wasn't right. Angus was never at a loss for words.

THE STRANGER

Clementine had been marking the calendar in the kitchen every afternoon, counting down the days until she and Aunt Violet would be going to the ballet. When Saturday morning finally arrived, she sat up in bed and counted the chimes from the grandfather clock in the downstairs hall.

'It's only six o'clock,' she said with a sigh. She pushed back the covers and scampered to her wardrobe.

Clementine had spent the previous evening trying to work out what she should wear, and in the end she still hadn't decided. Her mother had warned that she was becoming as fussy as Aunt Violet, but Clementine didn't mind. She wanted her outfit to be perfect.

The child ran her hand along the row of dresses until she came upon a navy smock with long sleeves. She pulled out some white tights and laid the ensemble on her bed, then took out a fluffy white vest from her chest of drawers. She settled on a spotted navy bow for her hair and, last of all, a pair of patent black boots.

'What do you think, Lavender?' Clementine consulted the pig, who was still snoring gently in her basket on the floor.

Clementine wrestled her arms into her dressing gown and then skipped down the main stairs to the lower landing. She stopped and looked up at her grandparents' portraits.

'I'm going to the ballet today,' Clementine informed the pair. 'Aunt Violet is taking me and, even though she won't say so, I think she's as excited as I am.'

Clementine could have sworn that her grandfather gave a little grin and Granny nodded. Even though they had both been gone for a very long time and Clementine had never met either of them in real life, she loved to tell them things.

She gave the pair a wave and shot off downstairs, skidding along the hallway into the kitchen, where her mother and Uncle Digby were already busy preparing breakfast for the guests. Quite some years ago, before Clementine had arrived, Lady Clarissa had opened Penberthy House as a country hotel. There were seven people staying in the house for the weekend, so it was just as well Clementine had asked Aunt Violet to take her to the ballet. Her mother had far too many things to do.

'Good morning, Mummy. Good morning, Uncle Digby,' the child said.

Digby Pertwhistle turned from where he was making a pot of tea. 'You're up bright and early, Clemmie.'

'It was the butterflies in my tummy. They woke me up.' Clementine climbed up on a chair at the kitchen table and poured herself some cereal.

'You've still got a few hours before you have to leave,' Lady Clarissa said. 'Why don't you put on some play clothes after breakfast and take Lavender and Pharaoh for a walk in the garden? I can call you when it's time to get ready.'

'What are you looking forward to the most?' Uncle Digby asked Clementine as he set the teapot on the table.

'The tutus and the twirling,' Clementine replied. 'Tilda said that they do lots of twirling.'

Uncle Digby and Lady Clarissa smiled at the child.

'I'm sure they do,' Uncle Digby said.

Clementine nodded. 'This is going to be the best day ever.'

Clementine squeezed Aunt Violet's hand as the train pulled into the station.

'Well, off we go,' the old woman said, steering the pair to their carriage. She led Clementine down the aisle, searching for the cleanest seats. 'Looks like this will have to do.'

Clementine went to sit down.

'Stop!' Aunt Violet commanded, and pulled a packet of antiseptic wipes from her navy handbag. She gave the vinyl seats and armrests a quick going over, then wiped them dry with a tissue.

'What's wrong, Aunt Violet?' Clementine asked. She didn't think the seats looked dirty at all.

'One can never be too careful, Clementine,' the woman replied, eyeing a man who was picking his nose further down the carriage. Aunt Violet shivered. 'Ghastly,' she muttered, and directed Clementine to sit beside the window.

'You look very nice today, Aunt Violet,' Clementine said. The woman was wearing a smart cream pants suit with navy accessories.

'Thank you, Clementine. These clothes are as old as the hills, which just goes to show that when you buy quality it lasts.'

Clementine grinned.

As the train sped through the countryside, Clementine stared out of the window. She picked out familiar objects and fired a volley of questions at her great-aunt about the sights she didn't recognise.

'Do you know the story of *Swan Lake*?' Aunt Violet asked after a while.

Clementine shrugged. 'A little bit. Tilda said that it's about a prince who wants to marry a swan that's not really a swan. She's really a princess who's under a spell.'

'Very good. Her name is Odette. And there's a nasty brute of a man called Von Rothbart who wants Prince Siegfried to marry his daughter instead,' Aunt Violet explained.

Clementine could feel her heart beating. 'What happens in the end?'

'Perhaps we should leave that as a surprise,' Aunt Violet said.

'I can't wait to find out,' Clementine sighed.

The train pulled into station after station, with more travellers getting on at each stop. Clementine wondered if everyone was going to the ballet.

A young man with curly brown hair dressed in black from head to toe sat down opposite them. Clementine noticed that he had a tattoo of a snake wriggling out from under his right sleeve and he was carrying a small black case.

Aunt Violet shuffled closer to Clementine and wrapped her arm protectively around the child.

'Do you think he's going to the ballet?' Clementine whispered.

'Don't be ridiculous.' Aunt Violet curled her lip. She hadn't travelled on the train for a very long time and wasn't especially enjoying the experience. It would have been her preference to drive but the city traffic always made her nervous.

'What's in there?' Clementine asked, pointing to the man's black case.

'I have no idea, Clementine,' the old woman breathed back. 'Just look out the window.'

'What's in your bag?' Clementine asked the fellow loudly.

'Clementine, it's rude to ask questions of strangers,' Aunt Violet sniped.

'Oh, this?' the young man said, placing the case on the seat beside him. 'It's for my work.'

'Good heavens,' Aunt Violet gulped and reached for Clementine's hand. She was imagining exactly what sort of work he did.

The young fellow unclasped the latches and opened the lid.

'It's an . . . oboe,' Aunt Violet declared as a wave of relief passed over her.

'Can you play it?' Clementine asked. She'd never heard of an oboe before and wondered what sort of sound it made.

The man smiled. 'Yes, but I don't think the other passengers would appreciate it right now,' he said, closing the lid again.

'We're going to the ballet.' Clementine's eyes widened. 'To see *Swan Lake.*'

'Really? It's a great production,' the man said, nodding. 'The dancers are lovely.'

'I'm sure you're very well acquainted with it,' Aunt Violet muttered and rolled her eyes.

The train's speakers crackled and a voice announced their arrival at the central station.

Clementine leapt from her seat and peered out at the platform. 'Are we here, Aunt Violet?'

'Yes, come along, Clementine,' the old woman said, taking her hand.

The young man picked up his case and stood up. 'I hope you enjoy the performance,' he said with a wink.

'We will.' Clementine grinned and waved goodbye as she and Aunt Violet hurried off the train.

SWAN LAKE

Clementine skipped along beside Aunt Violet as the pair navigated their way from the station to the opera house. A small crowd had gathered in front of the grand building. Clementine's eyes were everywhere as she took in the soaring columns, the enormous doors and the people in pretty dresses and smart suits.

Aunt Violet looked down at the girl. 'Ready?'

Clementine nodded, and they made their way into the building.

'Oh!' The child gasped as they entered the foyer. 'It's beautiful!'

'Yes, I suppose it is,' Aunt Violet replied. She'd almost forgotten how majestic the opera house was with its plush red velvet walls and gold fittings.

'Where do we have to go?' Clementine asked, trying to see through the growing mass of people.

Aunt Violet put on her reading glasses and retrieved the tickets from her purse.

'I think our door is around there,' she said, pointing to their right. 'We're miles away from the stage.'

'I don't mind,' the child replied. 'The most important thing is that we're at the ballet.'

Aunt Violet handed their tickets to the young usher on the door.

'I have to exchange these,' he said, producing an envelope from his pocket.

'What's wrong?' Aunt Violet snapped. 'Don't tell me there's been a mistake. We've come all the way from Penberthy Floss and I just don't see that we could turn around and do it all again another day.'

The young man with a shock of red hair and a dusting of freckles looked at the envelope, then back at Aunt Violet. 'Are you Miss Appleby?' he asked.

'Yes,' Aunt Violet replied crisply, wondering how he knew her name.

'You have been upgraded to a private box, just for the two of you,' he explained.

Clementine recoiled. Why did they have to sit in a box to watch the ballet? How would they see anything?

'Oh.' Aunt Violet's face lit up. 'Well, this is a surprise. Forget what I said about being miles away, Clementine.'

The young man noticed Clementine's discomfort. 'Is there something the matter, miss?'

'How big is the box?' Clementine asked. She hoped it was roomier than the cardboard box she and Sophie had made a cubby out of in the sitting room the last time Sophie stayed for a sleepover.

Aunt Violet and the usher looked at each other and grinned.

'Big enough,' Aunt Violet said with a twinkle in her eye. 'You'll see.'

Clementine frowned. She found that hard to believe but at least it was only for the two of them.

The young usher smiled at the pair. 'Someone will be up to collect you at the end of the performance.'

Aunt Violet frowned. 'What for?'

'I believe Miss Barkov has arranged something for you.'

Clementine's eyes sparkled as she wondered what Ana had in store for them.

'That sounds intriguing.' Aunt Violet looked at Clementine and raised her eyebrows.

The usher motioned for a girl with long dark hair to come over. 'Tasha, would you please show Miss Appleby and her granddaughter to their box?'

Clementine flinched. 'She's not my granny! She's my great-aunt.'

Aunt Violet rolled her eyes.

'But I wouldn't mind if she was my granny,' Clementine added quickly.

The old woman looked at the child. 'Do you mean that, Clementine?' she asked softly.

The child nodded, giving Aunt Violet's hand a squeeze. Aunt Violet smiled and squeezed her hand right back.

'Sorry,' the man said. 'I just thought . . .'

'Nothing to worry about, it was an easy mistake.' Aunt Violet nodded. 'And thank you.'

A few minutes later, having climbed a wide staircase with banisters so highly polished Clementine could see her own reflection in them, Tasha pushed open a door into a small balcony overlooking the stage.

Clementine's eyes almost popped out of her head. 'This isn't a box! It's a mansion.'

Three golden balconies, one above the other, wrapped themselves around the U-shaped theatre. There were rows and rows of red velvet seats, twinkling chandeliers and a vast red curtain hung across the enormous stage.

There were four seats in their private box. Clementine sat on the one closest to the stage, with Aunt Violet beside her.

They watched as the theatre filled with people, and it wasn't long until the *ding-dong* of bells rang out.

'What does that mean?' Clementine asked.

'It's to let everyone know that the performance is about to begin,' Aunt Violet said. 'People who turn up late have to wait until intermission to come in.'

Clementine looked at the old woman blankly.

'An intermission is a break in the middle of the performance for everyone to stretch their legs,' Aunt Violet explained.

'And go to the toilet?' Clementine asked.

'Godfathers! You don't need to go again, do you?'

The child shook her head.

The *plunk-plunk* of strings could be heard over the murmur of the audience. Clementine looked over the rail to see the orchestra tuning their instruments in a pit in front of the stage.

'Why are they in a hole?' Clementine asked. She studied the rows of instruments. 'Look, Aunt Violet! It's the man from the train.'

Clementine jigged about and pointed, but the old woman interrupted her. 'Shush, Clementine. Sit down! It's about to start.'

Clementine perched on the edge of her seat and stared over the balcony rail. A man dressed in a tail coat walked into the pit and stood on a platform. He bowed to the audience, who clapped loudly.

'He's the conductor,' Aunt Violet explained in a hushed tone. 'He's in charge of the orchestra.'

The man turned back to the orchestra and held a long skinny stick in the air. With a nod and a wave of his hand, the musicians began to play. The music was soft at first but steadily grew louder as more instruments joined in. After several minutes, there was a loud clash of cymbals, a rumbling of drums and then the curtain went up.

Clementine's jaw dropped as her eyes followed the dancers all over the stage.

'Where are the ballerinas?' she whispered. 'There are only boys.'

'Don't worry, the girls will be along shortly,' Aunt Violet whispered back. Sure enough, a group of young women in willowy dresses, and with garlands of flowers in their hair, danced onto the stage.

'Is it a party?' Clementine asked.

'It's a birthday party for Prince Siegfried,' Aunt Violet replied, her eyes not leaving the stage. 'Now just sit back and watch.'

OOPS!

Clementine stood up and leaned on the rail, mesmerised as the dancers pranced on and off the stage. She was amazed at how the scenes changed from the palace party to the lake in the blink of an eye. Aunt Violet glanced at the child a few times, wondering if she would lose interest but Clementine was captivated the entire time.

When the first act ended and the curtain came down, Clementine clapped loudly.

'I love it!' the child gasped, turning to Aunt Violet. 'How long until the next part?'

The old woman looked at her watch. 'We've got about fifteen minutes. I think we should take a trip to the ladies' room, then get a drink.'

Clementine nodded. 'Ballet makes me thirsty.'

Aunt Violet held Clementine's hand as they walked down to the bar in the foyer, stopping at the toilet along the way. There were people milling about, drinking champagne and loudly discussing what they'd seen so far.

'She's lovely but she's no Anastasia Barkov,' a round woman declared.

She was wearing a shimmery black top that billowed out like a tent and standing next to her was a slender man in a checked suit. They were waiting in line for the bartender, beside Clementine and Aunt Violet.

The woman looked down at Clementine. 'What do you think, dear?'

'Doris, she's a child,' the man scoffed. 'I'm sure she wouldn't have any idea what you're talking about.' He looked at Clementine. 'You've probably never even heard of Anastasia Barkov, have you?'

Clementine nodded. 'She's my ballet teacher and she lives at the end of our road.'

'Goodness, some children do have vivid imaginations,' the woman tutted.

'It's true,' Clementine said, wondering why the lady didn't believe her.

Aunt Violet had only just handed Clemmie a glass of lemonade with a fancy straw when the bells began their *ding-dong* chorus. They hurried back to their box, and Clementine watched as the theatre-goers made their way to their seats. She saw the lady in the shimmery top edging along a row down below and giggled when she almost landed in a man's lap.

The lights dimmed and the spotlight shone on the conductor as he walked into the orchestra pit and raised his stick.

Clementine couldn't wait to see what was going to happen next. She turned and smiled at Aunt Violet. 'Do you think it will all work out in the end?' the child asked. She didn't want the prince to fall in love with the wrong swan.

Aunt Violet nodded. 'I think it probably will.'

Clementine turned back to the stage and cradled her chin in her hands.

A little way into the performance, Clementine became distracted by the conductor. He was waving his arms furiously, his wild grey curls flying about. She peered down at the orchestra pit, where the musicians were concentrating hard on the sheet music in front of them. As Clemmie's eyes wandered back to the conductor, she noticed a page flutter off his music stand. The girl wondered if it was important.

All of a sudden, the music sped up. As it became faster and faster, the ballerinas and their partners raced around the stage. The musicians were reaching for the pages on their stands and turning them at great speed.

Clementine frowned. 'I think they skipped a bit,' she whispered to Aunt Violet.

'Shh, you mustn't talk,' the old woman chided.

When Clementine spotted one of the ballerinas spinning out of control on the side of the stage she was sure that something had gone wrong. But a minute later everything looked calm again.

Clementine wondered if the ballet always happened that way.

The evil sorcerer, wearing a black mask and cape, swept onto the stage. He danced around the lake and the swans, trying to keep Odette and the Prince apart. But it was no use, the pair leapt into the lake together, releasing Odette and the swans from their spell and causing the sorcerer to die. When Odette and her prince were at last united, the curtain fell.

Clementine clapped loudly and watched as the entire crowd rose to their feet. She looked at Aunt Violet, who was dabbing at her eyes with a handkerchief.

'Did you love it, Aunt Violet? I loved it so much,' Clementine gushed, standing up. 'Is that why you're crying?'

'Oh, don't be ridiculous. I've just got something in my eye, that's all,' the old woman blustered. 'Goodness knows how long it's been since they've dusted in here.'

But Clementine didn't believe a word of it.

A few minutes after the concert hall began to empty, Tasha knocked on the door and poked her head in. 'Hello,' she said brightly. 'Would you like to follow me, ladies?'

'Where are we going?' Clementine asked.

'Why don't we let Tasha surprise us, Clementine,' Aunt Violet suggested.

The young woman led the pair downstairs through a series of doors that were off-limits to the general public. It was a frenzy backstage with ballerinas running down the corridors, stagehands carrying equipment, and people with clipboards shouting into headsets.

'Just through here,' Tasha said as she pushed open another door.

Clementine held tightly to Aunt Violet's hand as the pair were ushered inside. A table in the centre of the room was weighed down with cake stands and platters of sandwiches. There was a small pile of plates and, off to the side, tea, coffee and a jug of lemonade.

'Everyone should be here soon,' Tasha said with a smile.

'Who's coming?' Clementine asked.

Tasha glanced at the sheet of paper in her hand. 'According to this, you'll be meeting the main characters and a couple of the musicians,' she replied.

Clementine gulped. 'Is the bad man coming too?'

'Yes, but he's not really a baddie. That's just part of the show. He's the sweetest one of all,' Tasha reassured her. 'I'll wait with you until they arrive.'

A moment later the door opened and Clementine hid behind Aunt Violet. A man dressed in black smiled and walked over to them. His feathered cape and scary mask were nowhere to be seen.

'Hello there,' he said. 'I'm Sean McCrae.'

'It's a pleasure to meet you, Sean,' Aunt Violet replied, holding out her hand. 'That was a marvellous performance.'

Sean peered over Aunt Violet's shoulder. 'And who do we have here?'

The old woman gave Clementine a little push.

'Hello,' the girl said shyly.

'You must be Clementine. Ana told me all about you. I'm bringing my wife and boys to your hotel in a couple of weeks' time. Did you enjoy the ballet?'

Clemmie nodded. 'Ana said you were coming to stay.'

'I have to get back upstairs,' Tasha said. 'Have fun, Clementine.'

'Thank you,' Aunt Violet said as the girl disappeared. Just as she was leaving, a group of ballerinas entered.

'Thank you,' Clementine echoed.

'Hello, you must be Miss Appleby and Clementine,' said the ballerina who played Odette. 'I'm Kat, and this is Lydia and Zizi. 'Sorry we're late.'

'It's a pleasure to meet you all,' Aunt Violet said, and Clementine gave a little wave.

'Would you like some lemonade?' Kat asked them.

'Yes, please,' Clementine said. 'You're such a good dancer.'

Kat smiled at the girl. 'Thank you, sweetie.'

'Please sit down, everyone. Sean's going to make us all some tea. Aren't you, Sean?' Zizi teased. 'Don't you think he should, after he spent all afternoon chasing us around the stage and scaring us half to death?'

Clementine giggled. 'He scared me too.'

'I'm sorry, Clementine. I didn't mean it. It's just my job.' The man grinned.

Zizi offered Clementine a scone with jam and cream. 'Is this your first visit to the ballet?' she asked.

Clementine nodded, sitting down beside Kat and her great-aunt. 'It was amazing! I tried to watch everyone and now my eyes hurt,' the child said.

The dancers laughed. The door opened and a woman with bright red hair walked through. There was another man behind her.

'This is Elaina, she plays the principal violin, and Toby plays . . .'

'The oboe!' Clementine burst out.

'Godfathers!' Aunt Violet almost choked on her tea.

'Aunt Violet, I tried to tell you I saw him in the hole in the floor.' Clementine smiled at the man.

'You're the little girl from the train.' The man grinned back at her. 'So did you like the performance?'

Clementine nodded. She took a sip of her lemonade then sat the glass back on the table. 'Was there a mistake after the intermission?'

The dancers and musicians looked at each other.

'Clementine, don't be silly,' admonished Aunt Violet. 'This is the *Royal* Ballet. They don't make mistakes.'

'What made you think there was a mistake?' Kat asked the little girl.

'I saw a page fall off the conductor's stand and then everything went really fast for a minute,' Clementine said.

The dancers and musicians exchanged glances and burst out laughing.

'You're absolutely right,' Sean said. 'The maestro missed a whole page and that's why we were racing about like headless chickens.'

'Really?' Aunt Violet scoffed. 'How extraordinary!'

'I looked up and wondered what the old boy was doing,' Toby said, shaking his head. 'I don't know how we kept it together. He didn't even realise until after the performance, when I picked up the sheet from the floor and handed it to him.'

'How did you know what to do?' Clementine asked.

'Well, we all sort of scrambled but, luckily, everyone was listening and watching,' Kat said. 'The show must go on, after all.'

'The maestro isn't the first to make a mistake and he won't be the last, I'm sure,' Toby said. 'I think he might be ready for retirement soon.'

'That's not the worst of it,' Lydia said. 'Do you remember the night my hair got caught in Sean's mask and we couldn't get separated? We had to dance for ten minutes while stuck together!'

Clementine giggled. 'That would be terrible.'

Sean and the others laughed.

'It wasn't *that* funny,' said Lydia, 'especially when they had to cut out a chunk of my hair to separate us.'

'Goodness, I had no idea so many things could go wrong onstage,' Aunt Violet said.

'Most of the time the audience never knows,' Kat confessed. 'You're amazing to have picked that up, Clementine. I think you're destined for a life on the stage.'

Clementine beamed.

The next half hour whizzed by. Clementine told the group about her ballet lessons and what she'd learned so far. Kat asked Clementine for a demonstration, and the girl was thrilled when Kat gave her a lesson on third position to show Ana on Monday afternoon. Clementine was sad when it finally came time to leave.

'Thank you so much for having us,' Aunt Violet said, standing up.

Kat rose from her seat and hugged Clementine goodbye. 'It was our pleasure. Tell Ana we said hello – we miss her very much.'

'And I look forward to seeing you at Penberthy House,' Sean added.

'Don't get your hopes up too much, Sean,' Aunt Violet said, then turned to Clementine. 'Well, what do you say?'

'Thank you. It was so lovely to meet you all,' the girl said.

'Oh, you're adorable, Clementine.' Lydia touched the child on the cheek and gave her another quick hug.

'Enjoy your ballet lessons, Clementine,' the girls chorused after her.

'And what should you always remember?' Sean called.

Clementine turned around and thought for a moment. 'The show must go on,' she said with a smile.

Sean grinned. 'That's right, Clementine. The show must go on!'

CONCERT PLANS

On Monday afternoon Clementine twirled into the hall, ready to learn as much as she could. She was glad to find Angus among the others.

'Hello Angus,' she said.

'Hi,' the boy replied quietly.

After the children had changed, Ana Hobbs directed them to sit down.

'Good afternoon, everyone,' Ana greeted the group. 'I've decided on your performance for the concert.'

The children clapped their hands and grinned.

'What is it?' Tilda asked. She and Teddy didn't even know what their mother had chosen.

'You're going to learn a very short and simple version of *Peter and the Wolf*.'

'I know that story,' Poppy said.

Ana smiled. 'Wonderful. For those who don't, it's a famous folktale about a boy named Peter who lives with his grandfather. One day, a hungry wolf comes to his garden and swallows a duck in one big gulp. With the help of a cat, a bird and some hunters, Peter bravely captures the wolf and takes it to the zoo.

'It's lucky that there are ten of you, because there are nine parts plus the narrator. But I think we'll add an extra hunter – it's a bit much to expect one of you to read the whole thing. Araminta will help us out there.'

Tilda and Teddy's big sister was standing next to the stereo. She wasn't especially keen on dancing herself but she was happy to help her mother with the lessons.

'Can I be the wolf?' Gareth asked.

'We'll see,' Ana said. 'Now, come closer so I can tell you about the characters and how they fit in with the music.'

The children wriggled forward.

'Every character is represented by a different instrument in the orchestra,' Ana began. 'There's a bird called Sasha and her instrument is the flute. Sonia the duck is represented by the oboe.'

Clementine's eyes widened. 'I know oboes,' she whispered.

Ana nodded. 'There's also Ivan the cat whose instrument is a clarinet; Peter with the string quartet; Grandpa with the bassoon; and the hunters are accompanied by the drums. And, of course, there's the wolf, whose instrument is the French horn. Now I want everyone to stand up and we'll do some warm-ups, then I'm going to get you to move like the characters and we can see who would like to be each part,' Ana instructed.

The children did some jumps and skips and moved through first and second positions.

Ana then stood on her tippy-toes and made fluttery movements with her arms. 'See if you can copy me and tell me which animal you think this is.'

The children all followed. 'It's the bird,' they called out.

'Her name's Sasha,' Sophie added.

'Would you like tó be her?' Ana asked.

Sophie nodded and fluttered her arms again.

Ana put her hands behind her bottom and began to waddle. The children copied her.

'That's Sonia the duck,' Clementine said. 'Please may I be her?'

Anna nodded. 'I think you would make a wonderful Sonia.'

The class continued following Ana's lead and it wasn't long before everyone had a part. Poppy was chosen to play the cat and Teddy was picked for the part of Peter. Tilda took the role of Grandpa, and Angus was appointed lead hunter with the two Kindergarten girls. That left Gareth to be the wolf.

Ana guided the children through the rehearsal. They worked on emphasising their movements and making sure they kept in time with the story. Clementine soon became an expert at waddling, and Ana suggested she do some leaps and twirls too. Clemmie was thrilled. She decided she would practise every day so that she could be just perfect.

The following Monday afternoon the children did a complete run-through of their production. Strictly speaking, it was more movement and drama than ballet, but Ana was delighted with their progress all the same. It was quite an achievement for them to remember so many moves in such a short amount of time. Though, little Gareth was a concern. The boy was often distracted playing with beetles or whatever else he'd managed to capture at school that day.

'How many more practices do we have?' Clementine asked.

'I've arranged for an extra one this Friday,' Ana replied. 'And then the concert is on Sunday.'

'That's not much time,' Clementine said. Her tummy began to feel like it was full of butterflies.

Ana nodded. 'That's why you all have to concentrate.'

Just as she said this, a tall man with a shiny bald head and a bushy beard arrived at the door. 'Hi there,' he called.

The children turned to look.

'Uncle Felix!' Teddy and Tilda raced over and launched themselves at him.

'Hello Felix,' Ana said as he walked towards her with his niece and nephew dangling from each arm.

He planted a kiss on Ana's cheek and set the children back down.

'I wasn't expecting you today,' Ana said.

'I finished it all sooner than I thought I would. Better to have it here for your rehearsals,' he replied with a grin.

'Absolutely, and it might help that little one visualise his role,' Ana whispered, pointing to Gareth, who was busy chasing a moth.

Ana introduced her brother Felix to the group. He gave the kids a wave then headed back outside. He soon returned carrying a huge sheet of timber in the shape of a forest, which he positioned on the stage. The children watched as the set came together. There was the cottage and the woods and a hill, all beautifully painted.

'Your uncle is good at making scenery,' Clementine said to Tilda.

Tilda nodded. 'He can build anything.'

'Are you going to watch us rehearse, Uncle Felix?' Teddy asked.

The man shook his head. 'I'm afraid not. I have to get back to the workshop and finish a few things. But I'll be here for the concert on Sunday.' He quickly said goodbye and gave the group a wave.

Ana turned back to the children. 'Well, what do you think?' she asked.

'It looks 'fressional,' Clementine said seriously.

Ana grinned. 'Do you mean professional?'

'Oops,' Clementine said, blushing. 'Sometimes I get big words mixed up. But Aunt Violet tells me.'

Ana could believe that. She mustered the children back into their places for another run-through.

Araminta was doing a wonderful job as the narrator. 'No sooner had Peter gone back into his house, than a big grey wolf came out of the forest . . .' the girl read aloud.

The children waited. The French horn played but there was no sign of the wolf.

'Gareth, it's time for you to come out of the woods,' Ana called gently.

Clementine waddled over to the trees and poked her head around. Gareth was completely mesmerised by the moth, which was flailing about trying to escape his sticky fingers.

'Gareth,' Clementine whispered. The boy ignored her, so she whispered louder. 'You're supposed to be chasing the duck,' she said crossly.

Gareth looked at her with big green eyes. 'Oh.'

He stood up and assumed his stalking position. Clementine danced away and Gareth finally appeared. It was just a pity the music was now miles ahead of where it should have been.

'Nice to see you, Gareth,' Ana said.

The boy smiled.

'Mintie, can we go back a bit, darling?' Ana called.

Araminta switched off the music and started it at the part where Gareth was supposed to come onstage. She read from the script again. 'No sooner had Peter gone back into his house, than a big grey wolf came out of the forest . . .'

This time Gareth rushed out snarling and growling, sending the rest of the cast flying.

Ana sighed. She hadn't realised that teaching ballet to five-year-olds would be like trying to herd cats.

TRIBBLE TROUBLE

Clementine, Sophie, Tilda and Poppy raced down onto the lower field, ready to join the lunchtime soccer game. As always, Joshua Tribble declared he was the boss because he brought the ball in from home.

'Okay, I'm the captain of the Missiles and –' Joshua looked around at the group of children standing in front of him – 'Clementine, you can be the captain of the other team. They're called the Stupid Piggy Wiggies.'

'No, we're not,' Clementine said. 'And pigs aren't stupid. My Lavender is really smart.'

'No, she's not. My goat could beat your pig any day,' Joshua challenged.

Clementine sighed. She wondered if she should ask Mr Smee for a ball from the sports room so they wouldn't have to do everything Joshua said.

'I'm choosing first,' Joshua announced, and pointed straight at Poppy.

Clementine was surprised that Joshua didn't pick Angus first. They were always on the same team. She chose Sophie, then Joshua picked Tilda. This went on until it came down to the last two – Angus and Astrid.

'Astrid, you're on my team.' Joshua pointed at the girl, whose eyes doubled in size.

Everyone was surprised. They knew Astrid would never actually kick the ball. She sort of hovered around it and ran away whenever it came towards her.

'How come I get Angus?' Clementine asked Joshua. She had deliberately not chosen Angus because she'd thought Joshua would get angry if she did. 'I'm happy he's on our team because he's a really good player,' she added.

'He's a loser,' Joshua said, and made an 'L' shape with his fingers on his forehead.

'He is not, and that's mean,' Clementine said.

Angus's face turned bright red and the boy turned and walked away.

'He is too.' Joshua pulled a face and grabbed the ball. He ran to the centre of the field and kicked off. 'No losers allowed on my team,' he shouted as he booted the ball to one of the boys.

Everyone except for Astrid raced after it like bees around a honeypot. She stayed back and ran to the other side of the field when the ball headed her way.

Joshua ran towards the goal. He kicked the ball to Eddie Whipple, who booted it straight past Sophie and into the net. The teams ran back to the centre and within a minute Joshua had scored again.

When Clementine finally got the ball, she kicked it to Angus, who sped down the sideline. Joshua and two other boys sprinted after him. Just as Angus was about to kick the ball, the three boys tackled him and the ball flew out. Clementine saw her chance and kicked the ball away.

'Astrid, watch out!' Clementine called as the projectile landed right in front of the other girl's feet.

Astrid stared at the ball as if it were about to turn into a fire-breathing dragon.

'Kick it, Astrid!' Poppy yelled from the other end of the field.

Astrid gulped. She looked at the goal and then at the boy standing in front of her, then she raised her leg and kicked it as hard as she could.

'No, not that way!' Poppy shouted. 'It's the wrong goal!'

The ball flew into the air. Clementine held her breath as it sailed into the back of the net.

Astrid looked as if she'd just seen Mrs Bottomley in a bikini.

Clementine, Teddy and the rest of their team raced over to the girl, cheering.

'Wow,' Astrid breathed. 'Did I just score a goal?'

Joshua Tribble ran into the group and snatched up the ball. 'Yeah, for the wrong team, doofus!' He ran back to the centre of the field. 'But we're still winning.'

Clementine turned to see where Angus had gone. The boy was sitting on the ground, where he'd lost the ball, his head in his hands. She ran towards him.

'Are you okay?' she asked, kneeling down beside him.

His face was streaked with tears and he was rubbing his shin. 'I'm fine,' the boy said bluntly, wiping his face with the back of his hand.

'Are you hurt?' Clementine looked at him.

Angus shook his head and stood up.

'Come on, crybaby,' Joshua teased. 'Are we playing soccer or doing ballet?'

Clementine's eyes widened. 'Is this all because you're doing ballet?' she asked Angus.

'I'm not doing stupid ballet anymore,' the boy snapped.

Clementine frowned. 'But we need you for the concert.'

'I don't care about the stupid concert and stupid ballet!' Angus shouted and raced away to the boys' toilets just as the bell rang.

MISSING

'Excuse me, Mr Smee.' Clementine looked up at the teacher as he was passing out handwriting books. 'Where's Angus?'

'He got a bump on his leg at lunchtime, so he's gone to get an ice pack and have a lie-down,' the teacher replied.

Clementine wondered if Angus had told Mr Smee what had happened.

'Yeah,' Joshua piped up from the next table and groaned. 'My foot's sore too. Angus kicked it.'

'Do you need an ice pack?' Mr Smee asked the boy.

Joshua shook his head. 'Nup. I'm way tougher than him.'

Clementine glared at the lad. She didn't believe that Angus's injury was an accident at all. And Joshua didn't seem to be having any trouble walking.

Angus stayed away from class for the rest of the afternoon, and he wasn't there on Friday morning when Mr Smee called the roll.

'Do you really think Angus is hurt?' Clemmie asked Sophie and Poppy.

The other girls shrugged.

'He might just have a cold,' Sophie said.

Clementine hoped that was it. She didn't like the thought of him being injured and, what's more, the last rehearsal for the concert was that afternoon. Angus had to come. He was the leader of the hunters and they wouldn't be very good without him.

After the children had eaten lunch and were dismissed from the dining room,

Joshua grabbed his soccer ball and raced to the oval, yelling at the other kids to hurry up.

'Come on, Clementine,' the boy shouted. 'I'll let you be a captain again.'

Clementine shook her head. 'I don't want to play.'

'Why not?' Joshua snapped.

'Because of what you did to Angus at soccer yesterday,' Clementine said crossly.

Joshua turned and ran back to her. 'I didn't do anything to Angus. Your boyfriend's a sissy-pants.'

'That's mean, Joshua, and it's not true. I'm going to tell Mr Smee what you did,' Clementine said. She hadn't noticed that the teacher was right behind her.

'What are you going to tell me, Clemmie?' Mr Smee asked. He'd seen Joshua standing with his hands on his hips and didn't think it was a good sign.

Clementine spun around, surprised to see him. Joshua narrowed his eyes but Clementine

wasn't scared. 'Yesterday at soccer Joshua was being mean to Angus,' Clementine said.

Roderick Smee frowned at Joshua.

'That's a lie,' the boy spat. 'She just wants to get me in trouble. He kicked me in the foot.'

'Joshua, we've talked about how important it is to tell the truth,' Mr Smee said sternly.

'You should talk to her about that,' Joshua said, pointing his finger at Clementine.

'I *am* telling the truth, Mr Smee.' Clementine took a deep breath. She could feel some bad butterflies in her tummy and there was a prickly feeling behind her eyes.

'Joshua, please stop pointing at Clementine and tell me what you believe happened yesterday,' the teacher instructed.

'Nothing,' Joshua lied. 'Angus and I were running for the ball at the same time and then he kicked me in the foot and he fell over.'

Two other boys standing beside him nodded and said that he was telling the truth.

Clementine felt hot. She didn't want Joshua to get away with being a bully.

'Well, I'll be speaking to Angus when he comes back to school on Monday,' Mr Smee said. 'Just to make sure.'

'Can we go now?' Joshua asked impatiently.

The teacher nodded, and the boys sprinted off towards the field. Clementine was left standing on her own.

'Aren't you going to join in?' Mr Smee asked.

Clementine shook her head. 'I don't want to,' she said.

'Clemmie, why do you think Joshua was being mean to Angus?' Mr Smee asked.

Clementine bit her lip. 'Because of ballet. Angus didn't want anyone at school to know he was doing ballet, but Joshua must have found out. He was calling Angus names yesterday and left him to be on my soccer team,' Clementine explained. 'He always picks Angus first.'

Mr Smee nodded. 'I see. Well, don't worry about it. I'll sort things out on Monday.'

Clementine nodded absently. With the concert on Sunday, Monday would be much too late. It was up to her to find a way to get Angus to the concert.

A PLAN

'Good afternoon, Clementine,' Aunt Violet greeted the child as she arrived at the school gate.

Clementine rushed forward and wrapped her arms around the old woman's waist.

'Heavens! To what do I owe such grand affection?' Aunt Violet frowned and gave the girl a squeeze back.

Clementine shrugged. 'Are we going to ballet practice?' she asked.

'Yes, I've got your things in the car,' the woman replied.

Clementine held Aunt Violet's hand and the two of them walked to the car, where Clementine climbed into the back seat.

Aunt Violet pulled out from the kerb and trundled along through Highton Mill until she reached the open road and planted her foot on the accelerator. She glanced in the rear-vision mirror at Clementine, who was staring out the window.

'A penny for your thoughts, Clementine,' she said.

'What?' The girl turned to look at her great-aunt.

'Clementine, please. "I beg your pardon" is the correct way to address someone if you don't hear them properly,' the old woman admonished. 'I said, "a penny for your thoughts", which means I was wondering what you were thinking.'

Clementine sucked in a deep breath.

'What's the matter, Clementine? I usually can't get a word in when I pick you up from school.'

Clementine looked at Aunt Violet through the gap in the seats, and sighed. She spent the rest of the trip to Penberthy Floss telling her about Angus and Joshua and her worry that Angus was sick and wouldn't come to the concert. Aunt Violet listened intently, and by the time they pulled up outside the village hall Clementine felt much better.

'Thank you, Aunt Violet,' she said as she hopped out of the car. 'If Angus doesn't come today I'm going to ask Mummy if I can talk to him on the telephone.'

'You know Sean and his family are coming to stay at the hotel tonight,' Aunt Violet said. 'Perhaps you could invite Angus over to play tomorrow. I'm sure Sean's boys would love a rowdy game of soccer on the back lawn. Perhaps Sean could join you and have a chat with Angus.'

Clementine thought for a minute, then her eyes grew wide. 'Aunt Violet, you're a genius!'

The old woman smirked. 'Yes, well, you just remember that.'

'Thank you.' Clementine reached in and hugged Aunt Violet before skipping off to join her friends.

'Places, everyone.'

Ana Hobbs clapped her hands together and the children scurried to the stage. Ana had enlisted Mrs Mogg's help to make some simple additions to the children's regular ballet outfits for the concert.

There were pointy ears and a tail for the cat, and a beak and fluffy wings for the bird. Clementine had the same for her part as the duck, except she wore a broad bill. The hunters held cardboard rifles and wore brown hats, Grandpa had a waistcoat and a bushy beard, and Peter wore a jacket and a hat and carried a coiled length of rope. The wolf had a long bushy tail and a mask that covered Gareth's whole head. Ana hoped that the boy would be able to see through it.

'Has anyone seen Angus?' Ana asked. The hunters were looking a little lost without their leader.

'He wasn't at school today,' Clementine said.

'Oh dear.' Ana made a note to telephone his mother after the lesson. She hoped he would be able to make it for the concert on Sunday. 'Remember, everyone, listen to the music and think about your actions – and, Gareth, please pay attention.'

The little boy nodded, sending his wolf head flopping forward.

Araminta stood at the microphone on the side of the stage, ready to start the narration. Ana turned on the music and the performance began. The children fluttered and waddled, skipped and twirled across the stage.

It was all running smoothly until Gareth came racing out of the woods, almost pushing Clementine off the stage.

'Gareth, stop, stop! It's wonderful you remembered to come on, but you need to be

a little bit less enthusiastic and a little more careful,' Ana cautioned the boy.

'But I couldn't see anything,' Gareth protested. 'This wolf head is too big.'

'Here, let me fix that for you.' Ana walked onstage and pulled the wolf head back, then secured it with a couple of bobby pins she took from her own hair. 'All right, we'll start again from the beginning.'

After the children had been through the dance five times, Ana decided to call it a day.

'Well done, everyone. I'm afraid that's it for our rehearsals,' said Ana. 'I need you all to be here by eleven o'clock on Sunday morning. We have to get you into your costumes and ready by midday.'

Araminta collected the various headdresses, tails and clothes from the children. There was a room at the back of the stage where Ana had arranged to store the costumes and set.

'We'll be like real ballerinas,' Sophie said with a beaming smile.

'Exactly!' Clementine nodded decisively.

'Oh, hello Mrs Tribble.' Ana spotted the woman near the door. 'We won't be long. I know you want to do some decorating for Sunday.'

'Yes, and the Irish dancing troupe is having their final rehearsal this evening too,' the woman replied.

Clementine looked around to see if Joshua was with his mother but there was no sign of the boy.

Ana would have loved to have an extra rehearsal with her group but apparently there was too much to do and everyone knew that Mrs Tribble was a woman on the edge of her nerves most of the time anyway. There was no point upsetting her.

'Is Mr Tribble coming to help you?' Ana said as the children ran to meet their parents.

'Yes, but we've had a little problem,' the woman said quietly. She fidgeted nervously. 'We've lost Herbert.'

'Oh, I'm sorry to hear it,' Ana said. She had no idea who that was and, given the seriousness of Mrs Tribble's voice, she didn't want to pry.

'Please let me know if there's anything I can do.'

Mrs Tribble sighed. 'I just wonder where he could be this time.'

Ana rounded up her charges and gave them some final instructions for Sunday morning.

'We're home,' Clementine called out as she raced through the back door and into the kitchen, with Aunt Violet following behind her.

Lady Clarissa looked up from where she was enjoying a quiet cup of tea before dinner. 'Hello darling.'

'Are the guests here?' Clementine asked.

'Would you like a drink, Clementine?' Aunt Violet offered. She walked over to the cupboard to retrieve a teacup.

'Chocolate milk, please,' Clementine said. She bent down to give Lavender and Pharaoh a scratch and a nuzzle.

'There's plenty of tea in the pot,' Lady Clarissa said.

'In answer to your question, Clementine, the McCraes have gone to dinner with Basil and Ana and the children.'

Clementine wrinkled her nose. 'Will they be home tomorrow?' she asked.

'Sean mentioned they would be here in the morning and they're going to spend the afternoon with the Hobbses. Don't worry, darling, you'll get to meet them.'

'Mummy, can you help me call Mrs Archibald, please?'

Lady Clarissa frowned. 'You mean Angus's mother?'

'Yes,' Clementine said.

'May I ask why?'

'Clementine has a plan,' Aunt Violet said as she placed the glass of chocolate milk in front of the child.

'A plan?' Lady Clarissa looked at Clementine, wondering what her daughter was up to this time.

'We have to get Angus to come to the concert on Sunday,' Clementine said. 'We need him. The other hunters aren't very good on their own.'

'Yes, having watched the dress rehearsal, I can vouch for that.' Aunt Violet's lip curled. 'And while you're rustling up performers, you'd do well to find a more reliable wolf too.'

Clementine nodded. 'Maybe Uncle Digby could do it.'

The kitchen door swung open and the old man walked through balancing a silver tray. 'What could I do?' he asked.

'Show your fangs and snarl a lot,' Aunt Violet said, taking a sip of tea. 'Nothing you don't do on a daily basis.'

'Aunt Violet!' Clementine smiled. 'No, he doesn't.'

Uncle Digby growled loudly and snapped his teeth.

Clementine giggled. 'Maybe a little bit.'

Aunt Violet's lips twitched as she tried very hard not to smile.

BREAK-IN

On Sunday morning Clementine and her mother arrived at the village hall right on eleven. The little girl's hair was pulled back into a bun and held in place with half a can of hairspray and a packet of bobby pins. She wore her red tutu with a white cardigan, white tights and beige ballet slippers.

Uncle Digby and Aunt Violet were coming later and Uncle Digby promised to bring Lavender in her tutu too.

Ana was there to meet them. 'You look wonderful, Clementine,' she said. 'Would you like to come with me and get your make-up done?'

Clementine nodded and shivered involuntarily.

'Are you cold, darling?' her mother asked.

The child shook her head. 'No, I'm excited.'

They followed Ana inside and were shocked by the hall's transformation.

'It's lovely,' Clementine exclaimed.

Bunting in pretty patterns of red, white and blue was strung diagonally across the room, and thick black curtains hid the stage. There were rows of new seats and a shiny black piano in the corner that had only been delivered the afternoon before. Basil Hobbs was standing at the back positioning a huge video camera on a tripod. He looked up and gave a wave.

An exhibition from Mrs Mogg's quilting group was hung up around the room. Off to the side of the main hall was the servery with the kitchen behind. In another smaller area, the afternoon tea was being set up by

Mrs Tribble. Father Bob was busy arranging a huge bunch of roses from his garden to fill the vase in the centre of the long table.

Mrs Mogg gave Lady Clarissa and Clementine a wave from the kitchen.

'If you don't mind, Ana, I think I should give Mrs Mogg a hand,' Lady Clarissa said.

'Yes, of course,' Ana replied. 'It won't take long to get the children ready – there are only a few props and Mintie's made a start on the make-up.'

Sophie and Poppy arrived and headed off with Clementine. Teddy and Tilda were already out the back with their sister.

Soon the little room was full of excited children. When Clementine's make-up was finished she stood by the door watching and waiting and, most of all, hoping.

All of a sudden she rushed out into the hall.

'Angus!' she cried, throwing her arms around the boy.

Angus's freckles exploded into crimson confetti.

'I'm so glad you came,' Clementine said. 'I knew you'd listen to Sean when you came over to play yesterday.'

The boy smiled. 'Well, he was a pretty good soccer player and if he can play soccer and do ballet, so can I,' he said.

Over Angus's shoulder, Clementine spotted Joshua Tribble arrive with his father. She didn't want Angus to see him, so she grabbed the lad by the hand and quickly dragged him out the back to get ready.

'Mrs Mogg made you a little hat and you have a rifle too,' she explained on the way. 'They're in the room behind the stage. But Mintie's doing make-up first.'

Angus flinched. 'I'm not wearing make-up!'

He reluctantly followed Clementine into the room, where he was greeted with great enthusiasm.

'I'm very glad to see you, young man,' Ana said with a smile. 'The girls were a bit lost without their lead hunter.'

'We thought you were sick,' Poppy said.

Angus shrugged.

Ana hadn't been able to get hold of Angus's mother but Sean McCrae had told her that she should expect the boy.

Ana gave Clementine a wink and mouthed 'thank you'.

Clementine beamed.

'Well, come on, everyone,' Ana said. 'Time to get the rest of your costumes on.'

The children followed their teacher to the storage room.

'Oh no!' Ana gasped. 'What on earth has happened in here?'

The children gasped too. Their lovely costumes were strewn all over the floor. Clementine picked up her duck bill, which was now flattened and torn. One of her wings was broken and half the feathers were missing too.

'Look at my hat,' Tilda moaned. It was crumpled and, on closer inspection, looked as if it had bite marks on it.

'Who could have done this?' Araminta said.

'Someone must have broken into the hall,' Teddy said, holding up his waistcoat. It was missing a pocket and all of its buttons. 'We have to catch them.'

Ana looked around. 'We'll have to worry about that later. I'm afraid there's no time to fix anything before the concert.'

The children heard the hall's speakers crackle to life.

'Good afternoon, everyone, and welcome to the official opening of the Penberthy Floss Village Hall,' came Father Bob's voice. 'It's lovely to see so many of you here this afternoon. There's a range of wonderful entertainment for us all today, followed by a delicious afternoon tea.'

'You have to go on in a few minutes,' Ana whispered to the children.

'Where's my wolf head and tail?' Gareth grouched.

While the rest of the cast still had bits and pieces of their costumes, Gareth's seemed to have disappeared altogether.

'That was the best costume,' Sophie said unhappily. 'It must have been stolen.'

Ana sighed.

Clementine looked around. Her throat felt funny, like there was a big lump of disappointment stuck inside. It wasn't fair that their lovely costumes were ruined. But then she remembered something she'd learned at the ballet.

Suddenly, Clementine smiled. 'It doesn't matter about the costumes,' she said loudly. 'The show must go on.'

'You're absolutely right, Clementine.' Ana nodded decisively. 'Okay, everyone, let's get up onstage. I'll tell Mrs Mogg what happened to her beautiful costumes later. I hope she's not too upset.'

Gareth sat down in the corner. 'I'm not going,' he said. 'I want my wolf head!'

'Come on, Gareth, you'll be a great wolf without it,' Ana coaxed the boy.

'No!' He shook his head stubbornly. 'I'm not doing it!'

Ana bit her lip.

'We'd like to welcome to the stage our very first performance of the day,' Father Bob continued. 'You may have heard that we now have the pleasure of a world-renowned prima ballerina living in our village. Ana Hobbs has only been teaching ballet in the hall for a few short weeks but we are about to have a very special treat. Her junior class is going to present an abridged version of the classic tale of *Peter and the Wolf*.'

The audience burst into applause and someone whistled.

'Come along, everyone.' Ana bustled her ragtag cast onto the stage.

Gareth refused to budge. Araminta zipped across to the far side to take her place at the microphone, which was positioned in front of the curtains.

Clementine glanced at the little house and the woods and realised that the chimney was half gone and the trees were all chewed around the edges.

'Look, Ana,' Clementine whispered and pointed.

'Oh dear, how did that happen?' Ana frowned. This truly was bizarre. 'Well, there's nothing we can do about it now.'

She pressed 'play' to start the music and pulled on the cords to open the curtains. Ana looked across at Araminta and nodded.

'This is the story of Peter and the Wolf,' the girl began. 'Each character in the tale is represented by a different instrument in the orchestra. For instance, the bird will be played by the flute, like this . . .'

Sophie fluttered across the stage. Her broken beak looked as if she'd flown off-course and into a glass door. The feathers on her left arm were falling like snowflakes but she fluttered as well as ever.

'What's happened to Sophie's costume?' Aunt Violet whispered, arching an eyebrow. 'Godfathers, look at Clementine. That duck bill looks as if it's been under a steamroller.'

A murmur ran through the audience.

'What's wrong with that chimney?' a man in a brown checked suit said loudly.

Uncle Felix frowned. 'That's not how I made it,' he said.

But the children continued as if nothing was wrong at all. When Araminta got to the part where she was to introduce the wolf, Gareth was nowhere to be seen. So she left him out and hoped he'd appear later on. It seemed silly to be doing a performance of *Peter and the Wolf* without the wolf.

'Are the children's costumes meant to be some sort of modern statement?' Mr Mogg asked loudly.

His wife elbowed him in the ribs. 'No, Clyde. Something must have happened to them,' she said through gritted teeth.

Mr Mogg chuckled. 'They look like they've been chewed by a goat if you ask me.'

At the mention of the word 'goat', Mrs Tribble gulped and stiffened in her seat.

'Angus looks stupid,' Joshua said.

His father gave him a glare that would freeze fire. 'You keep quiet, young man. I think Angus is doing a very good job up there,' Mr Tribble hissed. 'He looks like a brave hunter to me. If you'd been a bit braver, we might not have lost Herbert.'

Joshua folded his arms and pouted. It wasn't his fault that the beast chased him through the open gate.

Despite their scrappy costumes and the chewed set, the children were doing a marvellous job.

Everyone was keeping time with the music, which had just reached the point where the wolf was to appear. Ana hoped that Gareth had changed his mind and had decided to join in when she spotted something completely unexpected.

'Oh no,' she gasped. 'What is that?'

A GOAT IN WOLF'S CLOTHING

'No sooner had Peter gone than a big grey wolf came out of the forest,' Araminta continued.

From the corner of the stage, a four-legged creature with the head of a wolf wobbled onto the stage. Except it wasn't grey. It was cream-coloured with patches of brown.

'That's not Gareth!' Tilda whispered loudly. The dancers spun around and faced the beast.

'Look, it's a real wolf!' someone in the audience shouted.

'No, it's not – there are horns poking out of those ears,' Uncle Digby called. Lavender, who was sitting on his lap, grunted in agreement.

There was a roar of laughter, which startled the beast and sent it skittering across the stage.

'Watch out!' Angus cried as the creature crashed into the forest. The trees swayed, and Teddy and Poppy just managed to catch them before they fell over.

The little girls who were playing the other hunters dropped their rifles and ran offstage, squealing.

'Joshua Tribble,' Father Bob yelled above the ruckus, 'is that your missing Herbert?'

The creature bleated loudly. 'Baaaaa!'

'It's a goat!' Clementine called.

Clyde Mogg nudged his wife. 'See, I told you it looked like those costumes had been chewed by a goat.'

'Well, don't just sit there.' Aunt Violet glared at the people around her. 'Somebody catch it!'

'Why don't *you* catch it!' the old man in the checked suit snorted.

Onstage the music was still playing but by now the children had completely lost their place.

'I'll get him.' Angus, the brave hunter, launched himself at the goat. Herbert began to buck and bleat and for a moment it looked as though he and Angus were both heading for Aunt Violet's lap.

'Get it away from me!' the old woman yelped.

Lavender leapt down from Uncle Digby's knees and trotted under everyone's chairs and up the stairs onto the stage. She pranced around the goat as if she were trying to round him up.

'Don't just sit there, son,' Mr Tribble roared. 'He's *your* goat!'

Joshua gulped and raced onto the stage. 'Give me that!' he yelled, pointing at the rope slung over Teddy's shoulder. Joshua did his best to make a lasso.

Poor Angus was holding on for dear life as Herbert dragged him around the stage with Lavender snuffling at his feet. All of a sudden the beast changed course and was heading straight for Clementine.

'Look out, Clementine!' Angus yelled, but the girl was having none of it. No silly goat was going to ruin her first ballet performance.

'Stop!' Clementine scolded Herbert, holding up her hand. The audience gasped as the creature screeched to a halt. She eyeballed the wolf head.

'Careful, Clementine, he's got a good set of horns,' Uncle Digby called out.

'Oh dear,' Lady Clarissa whispered as her heart skipped a beat.

Joshua had just enough time to slip the rope over the goat's neck.

'Bravo, Clementine! Bravo, Lavender and Angus!' Aunt Violet cheered. Uncle Digby clapped loudly and so did the rest of the audience.

Ana sighed. 'Well done, children.'

'And I've got it all on tape,' Basil piped up from the back of the room and grinned widely.

The hall erupted into laughter.

Despite the commotion, the music continued to play and had just reached the part where the hunters and Peter were taking the wolf off to the village so it could be put into the zoo.

Joshua held tight to the rope while Angus had his arm around its neck. Clementine looked out into the audience and spotted Sean and his family. He gave her a big thumbs up.

Clementine beckoned for Sophie, Poppy, Tilda and Teddy to join her, and even the two little Kindergarten girls came back onstage.

'Remember,' Clementine whispered loudly, 'the show must go on.' She turned and nodded at Araminta.

The girl frowned then realised what Clementine wanted her to do. She quickly resumed her position at the microphone.

The audience members smiled as the children danced and pranced in a line in front of Herbert and his captors, keeping far enough away from his horns. Clementine waddled and quacked even though she was supposed to be in the wolf's tummy, and Sophie fluttered her wings as Araminta read the final lines. Lavender walked along with them too.

'Above them flew Birdie, chirping merrily. "My, what brave fellows we are, Peter and I! Look what we have caught!"'

The audience went wild. Clementine and the children who weren't holding onto Herbert curtseyed and bowed just as Ana had taught them.

Herbert looked out into the audience and bleated loudly. 'Baaaaa!'

'Well done, Angus! Good work, Joshua!' a voice called. Clementine was surprised to see it was Mr Smee.

Joshua grinned. He looked over at Angus. 'Sorry about what I said,' the boy whispered. 'And for what happened at soccer.'

'It's okay.' Angus shrugged. 'I'm quitting anyway.'

Clementine spun around. 'No, you can't. We need you,' she said.

Joshua nodded. 'You should keep doing ballet.'

'But you'll just tease me,' Angus said. 'And you won't be my friend anymore.'

Joshua shook his head. 'No, I won't. We'll always be friends.'

Clementine hoped that was true.

In the back room Gareth heard the clapping and cheering and finally decided to come out. He crept onto the side of the stage, following a trail of brown pebbles.

'Who dropped the chocolates?' The boy leaned down and picked one up. He was just about to pop it into his mouth when the audience gasped.

'No!' they all called at once.

'Hey, that's my wolf head!' the little boy cried out, spying Herbert. The dropping fell out of his hand and back onto the floor.

Everyone roared with laughter.

'I think someone found your costume out the back last night. Poor goat's probably starving if it's had that thing on its head for a while,' Mr Mogg said.

Father Bob stepped up to the microphone.

'Thank you, children. That's certainly one performance we'll never forget. It was unexpected but absolutely marvellous. And well done, Clementine – who knew that on top of being a wonderful waddler and twirler you are also a goat whisperer too. We'll give the children time to exit the stage and then I believe next on the program we have an Irish dancing demonstration. Mr Tribble, I wonder if you'd be so kind as to take Herbert off Joshua's hands?'

Angus and Clementine looked at the lad.

'I need to change my shoes,' Joshua mumbled sheepishly.

'What for?' Angus asked.

'Come on, Joshua,' a pretty blonde woman called. 'Hurry backstage, the rest of the group is waiting for you.'

Clementine's eyes widened. 'Do you do Irish dancing?' she asked.

Joshua nodded.

'So that's what you were doing in the locker room at school the other day.'

'He's a champion in the making,' Mrs Tribble said proudly.

Joshua's face went bright red. 'Muuuum, stop it, you're embarrassing me,' he said through gritted teeth.

'Go on,' Mrs Tribble said to the boy.

Joshua scurried offstage.

Clementine smiled, and Angus did too.

Mr Smee looked up from the audience and gave them both a wink.

CAST OF CHARACTERS

Clementine Rose Appleby	Five-year-old daughter of Lady Clarissa
Lavender	Clemmie's teacup pig
Lady Clarissa Appleby	Clementine's mother and the owner of Penberthy House
Digby Pertwhistle	Butler at Penberthy House
Aunt Violet Appleby	Clementine's grandfather's sister
Pharaoh	Aunt Violet's beloved sphynx cat

Friends and village folk

Margaret Mogg	Owner of the Penberthy Floss village shop
Clyde Mogg	Mrs Mogg's husband
Claws Mogg	Margaret's tabby cat
Father Bob	Village minister
Odette Rousseau	Sophie's mother
Mr Tribble	Joshua's father
Mrs Tribble	Joshua's mother
Herbert Tribble	Joshua's goat
Mrs Archibald	Angus's mother
Basil Hobbs	Documentary filmmaker and neighbour
Ana Hobbs (nee Barkov)	Former prima ballerina and neighbour

School staff and students

Mrs Ethel Bottomley	Teacher at Ellery Prep
Mr Roderick Smee	Clementine's Year One teacher
Sophie Rousseau	Clementine's best friend
Poppy Bauer	Clementine's friend, classmate
Araminta Hobbs	Ten-year-old daughter of Basil and Ana
Teddy Hobbs	Five-year-old twin son of Basil and Ana, classmate
Tilda Hobbs	Five-year-old twin daughter of Basil and Ana, classmate
Angus Archibald	Friend in Clementine's class
Joshua Tribble	Boy in Clementine's class
Astrid	Clever Year One girl

Others

Sean McCrae	Guest at Penberthy House and friend of Anna Hobbs
Felix Barkov	Anna Hobbs's brother
Gareth	Member of Clementine's ballet class
Toby	Oboist
Tasha	Usher
Kat, Lydia, Zizi	Ballerinas
Elaina	Principal violinist

ABOUT
THE AUTHOR

Jacqueline Harvey taught for many years in girls' boarding schools. She is the author of the bestselling Alice-Miranda series and the Clementine Rose series, and was awarded Honour Book in the 2006 Australian CBC Awards for her picture book *The Sound of the Sea*. She now writes full-time and is working on more Alice-Miranda and Clementine Rose adventures.

www.jacquelineharvey.com.au

Look out for Clementine Rose's next adventure

CLEMENTINE ROSE

and the Movie Magic

1 April 2015